CHAMPAK

AF527861

That's Not Right

MOONSTONE

Published in Moonstone
by Rupa Publications India Pvt. Ltd 2024
7/16, Ansari Road, Daryaganj
New Delhi 110002

Sales Centres:
Bengaluru Chennai
Hyderabad Jaipur Kathmandu
Kolkata Mumbai Prayagraj

P-ISBN: 978-93-6156-413-0
E-ISBN: 978-93-6156-642-4

First impression 2024

10 9 8 7 6 5 4 3 2 1

Printed in India

Kite Away

Circle the unusual things at the kite flying festival.

That's Not Right

Beach Buddies

Circle the things that you find funny on the beach.

That's Not Right

Spot the activities that are good for the environment.

Girl Power

Circle the famous personalities playing the sports.

That's Not Right

March 8 is Women's Day

Animals' Day Out!

Name the games you think the animals are playing.

That's Not Right

Nurse Pulse

Circle the funny things at the hospital.

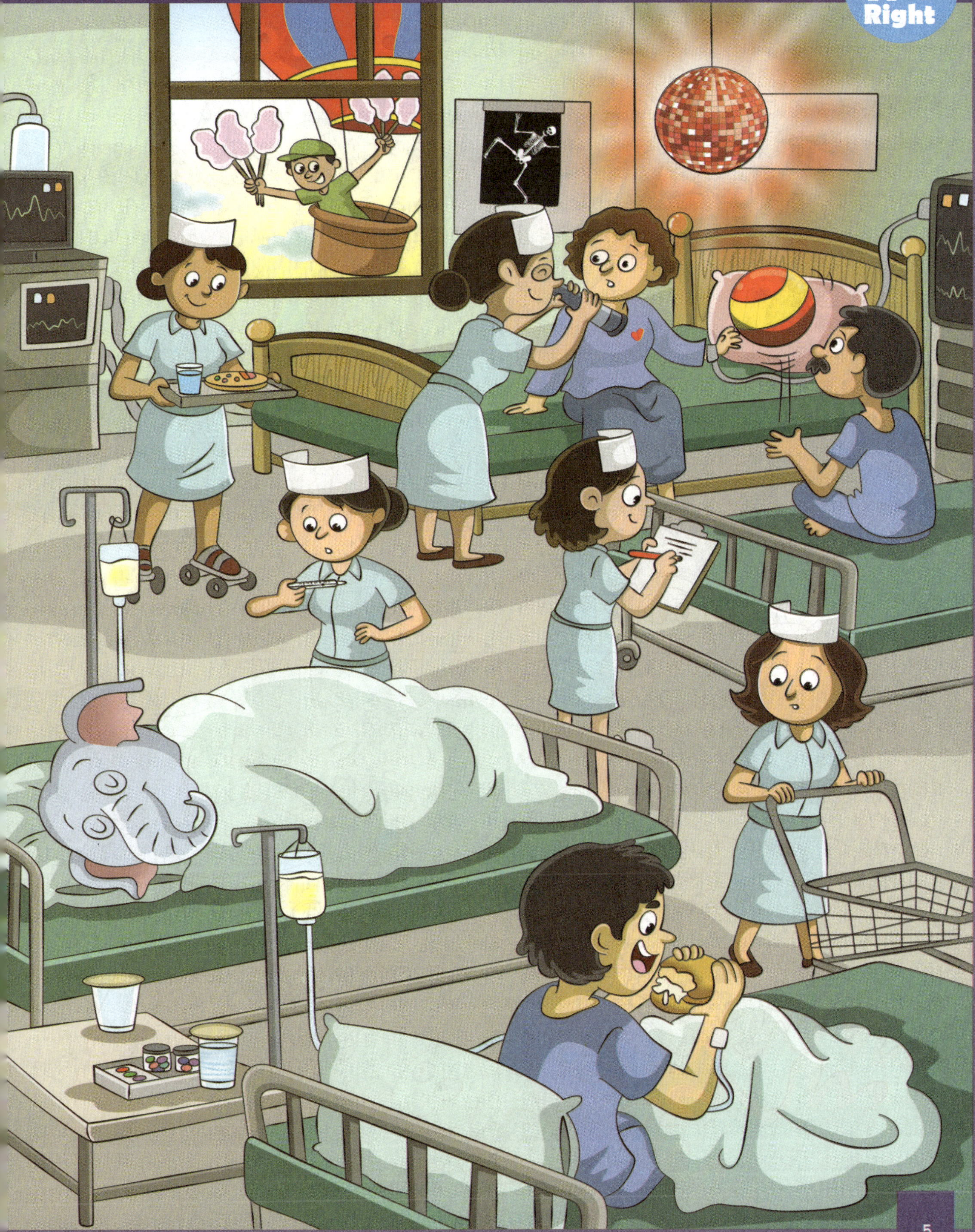

Tennis Menace!

Spot and circle the strange things at the tennis match.

That's Not Right

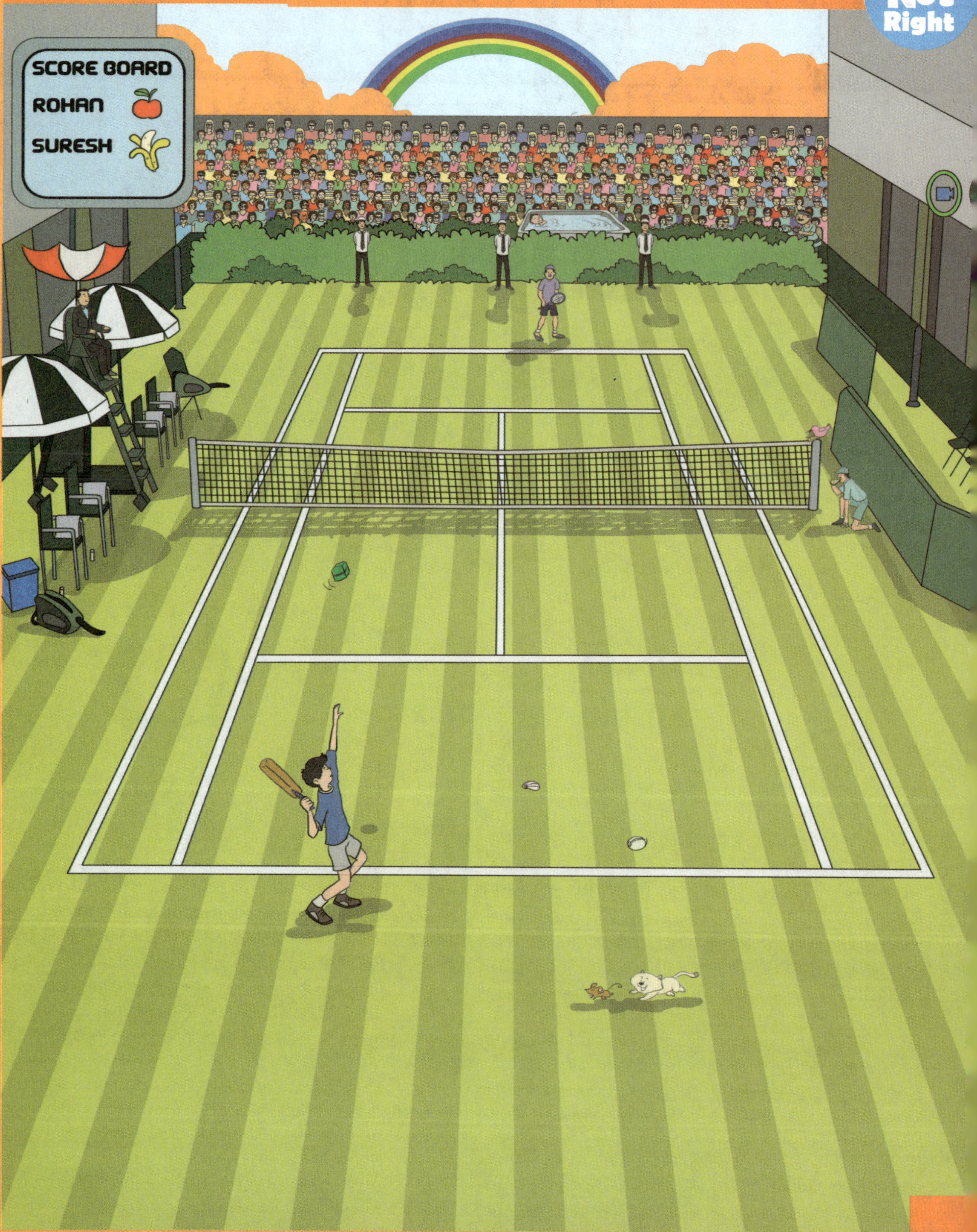

Monsoon Fun!

Circle the things that are fun to do on a rainy day.

Jungle Spy

Circle the things that you find funny in the jungle.

That's Not Right

Label the animals as herbivores or carnivores.

Greenhouse Play!

How many types of flowers can you spot? Count them.

That's Not Right

Find a reptile

Snowed In

Ishaan's family is enjoying the winter day. Circle the things that are not done in winter.

Doll Display

Circle pairs of similar looking dolls in the picture.

That's Not Right

Arctic Magic

It's cold here. Pick characters from the scene, and make up a funny story to laugh out loud!

That's Not Right

Percy bear was painting his house red when Piku penguin kicked his bucket of paint.

Crossed

Circle and name all the vehicles that you can spot in the picture below.

What job does the monkey have here?

Summer Play

Circle all the sports-related things you can spot in the picture. Name the sport they are used for.

That's Not Right

Stay on the track!

Cross out the things that are not found at the railway station.

That's Not Right

Tricolour Day! Spot and circle the things with the colours of the Indian flag.

That's Not Right

Trick & Treat!

Count the number of pasta at the Halloween party!

That's Not Right

Arctic Magic

Circle the activities you like during the winter.

That's Not Right

Zoo Much Fun

Circle the things that you find funny in this zoo.

That's Not Right

Circle the things that are not right in this picture.

That's Not Right

Silly Street

Cross out the things that don't belong on a busy signal.

That's Not Right

Sea Shenanigans

Spot and circle the things that are not found underwater.

Cool School

Count the number of snacks and check if each student will get one.

That's Not Right

Circle your favourite summer activities

That's Not Right

Farm Chores

Circle all the animals that are found on the farm.

That's Not Right

Neighbourhood

Count the number of windows and balconies in the neighbourhood.

That's Not Right

The Grandparent Gala

Which grandparents are having fun in the grandparent gala? Circle them.

That's Not Right

Football Fix

Circle the things that don't belong on a football field.

That's Not Right

Wild, Wild Camp!

Circle the things that you find funny at the summer camp.

That's Not Right

Which activity would you like to do?

Stretched

Count the people who are doing the upward stretch correctly.

That's Not Right

Rocky Road

Circle the things that belong on the busy road.

That's Not Right

Ferris Wheeling!

Count the number of children in the picture below.

That's Not Right

Feastin' Glee!

Circle the things that don't belong in a restaurant.

Clash of Worlds

Count the number of coffee mugs in the picture below.

That's Not Right

Midnight Mischief

Circle the things that you find funny in the midnight scene below.

That's Not Right

Baker Chaos!

Circle the things that belong in a bakery.

Count the number of berths in the train coach.

Circle the things that look odd for snow-capped hills.

That's Not Right

Who's At The Table?

Spot and circle the things that look funny to you.

That's Not Right

Which table has seafood on it?

Birthday Bash

Count all the animals at the birthday party.

Racer Fever

Circle the odd one out on the race track.

That's Not Right

Lib-Crazy!

Count the number of blue books in the library.

That's Not Right

What is the name of the board game shown here?

Museum Madness

Circle the things that belong to the 'Natural Science' section.

That's Not Right

Puddle In! Circle the things that look odd in the rainy day below.

That's Not Right

Circus Fuss!

Spot and circle the things that belong to a circus show.

That's Not Right

Amusing Park

Circle your favourite activities in the amusement park.

That's Not Right

Party Pitch

Spot and circle: 'Vegetable vendor', 'The Umpire' and 'An Astronaut'

That's Not Right

Crossover Classroom

What board game are the birds playing?

That's Not Right

 Circle the things that make noise.

A Zoo at Odds

Circle your favourite animals in the zoo.

That's Not Right

School's Out!

What is the schoolgirl buying from the stall? Who else is eating the same thing?

That's Not Right

Circle the student who is wearing the wrong uniform.

Banker's World! Circle the things that don't belong in a bank.

That's Not Right

Firefighter Might!

Spot the odd one out among the firefighters.

That's Not Right

Fish Market

Besides fish, count the other things being sold at the market.

That's Not Right

Navratri Joy

Circle the things that are found at a Dandiya Raas dance night.

That's Not Right

Lights, Crackers, Festival!

What are the fun things about this Diwali gala.

That's Not Right

Station-Smarter

Circle the things that are found at a railway station.

That's Not Right

Tea-ming up!

Cross out the things that are found in the tea garden.

That's Not Right

(Mis)Match

Cross out the wrong things on the cricket pitch.

That's Not Right

Machine Doctor!

Count the number of radios and circle the funny helpers.

That's Not Right

Aquariummm...

How many ice creams is the octopus eating?

That's Not Right

Chefs At Work

Circle the funny things in the kitchen.

That's Not Right

Park Question-Mark

Circle the things at the picnic that you find silly.

That's Not Right

Rock-Stars

Circle the things that are essential for rock climbing. Can you name them?

That's Not Right

At the Assembly

Cross out the animals at the assembly.
Count the number of children praying.

That's Not Right

Help the Doctor!

Circle all the funny things in the doctor's office.

That's Not Right

Build Me Up!

Circle the things that are commonly found at a construction site.

That's Not Right

Kai Po Che!

Count the kites in the picture. Circle your favourite one.

That's Not Right

Suitcase Race!

Cross out the things you will not find on the luggage belt.

That's Not Right

Get, Set, Oh No!

Circle the different sports being played at the stadium.

That's Not Right